THE SEVEN PRINCIPLES OF KWANZAA

NGUZO SABA

Umoja unity

Kujichagulia self-determination

Ujima collective work and responsibility

Ujamaa cooperative economics

Nia purpose

Kuumba creativity

Imani faith

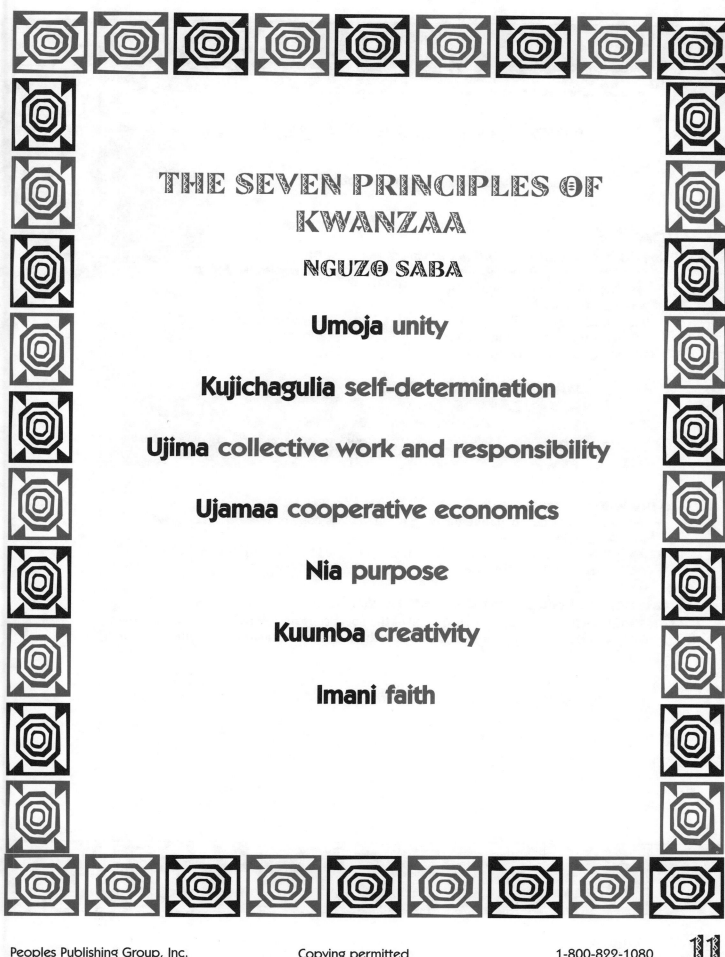

GRADES 2-3

MUFARO'S BEAUTIFUL DAUGHTERS
by John Steptoe
Illustrated by John Steptoe

GOAL

Using the book *Mufaro's Beautiful Daughters*, pupils will:

demonstrate **receptive language** in Mainstream American English (MAE) by:

- engaging in verbal and written activities,
- reading aloud,
- using writing skills,
- learning note-taking skills,
- analyzing a character in the story.

MATERIALS TO PREPARE

for each pupil in the group,

- a copy of ***Mufaro's Beautiful Daughters***
- a copy of the note-taking **copy master** at the end of this lesson
- the **poem copy master** at the end of this lesson

to use with the group,

- if a copy is not available for each pupil, a class copy of ***Mufaro's Beautiful Daughters***
- **globe** or **map** of Africa with Zimbabwe labeled so that pupils can find it
- **class chart** or **chalkboard**

Materials to Prepare for Cross Curricular Links

LANGUAGE ARTS a copy for each pupil of the poem copy master at the end of this lesson
GEOGRAPHY   globe, or map of Africa with Zimbabwe labeled so that pupils can find it, paper

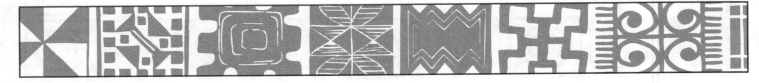

PART 1 INTO the Lesson

INTRODUCTION

Discuss the concepts of balance, fairness, and justice.

In your family and with your friends, how can you be fair?

If people do not agree with each other, how can you help to be fair and balanced with the people you care about?

Continue the discussion of these difficult concepts. Perhaps pupils have tried to be fair in helping care for younger children. (Note: Be careful to guide the discussion so that you do not lead pupils to violate family privacy, such as inappropriate discussions of balancing parents who disagree.)

What is justice?

What do balance and fairness have to do with justice?

Be sure pupils understand that the concept of justice extends beyond what their opinion of personal fairness might be.

We will read a story in a few minutes in which Manyara has to think very carefully about justice. To help you remember and think about the story, we are going to learn a new skill, note-taking. Note-taking means writing down words or drawing pictures that will help you remember whatever you think is important.

Have you ever taken notes?

Encourage pupils to recall and share any ways they have used written or other cues to help them remember something.

Note-taking can help you understand and enjoy something you want to understand, such as the story. Here is a note-taking page you may use as we read the story. Look at the note-taking page.

Distribute copies of the note-taking copy master at the end of this lesson. Tell pupils that the main character of the story is named Manyara, and that the note-taking sheet will help them to think about her. She is a complicated character. Tell pupils that, after reading the story and taking notes, the notes will be shared and the group will discuss Manyara. Explain that the goal of the note-taking sheet is to help them note details in the story that tell them about the character Manyara and what she is like.

INTRODUCTION Cont'd...

PREREADING

Next, introduce the book to pupils.

We are going to read a book about a special girl named Manyara. She is a complicated and beautiful African girl, as complicated and beautiful as each one of you.

Have pupils help you read the book's name and the names of the author and illustrator. Explain that the book is about a girl in Africa. Show pupils a map of Africa. Discuss how large Africa is, and that it is not a country, but a continent. Explain that a continent has many countries on it. Help pupils find Zimbabwe, the country in which the book is set.

Show pupils the book's cover and a few pages in the book.

What do you think the story will be about?

You may wish to record pupils' predictions on the chalkboard or class chart for review after reading the story.

Chalkboard

English For Your Success
Curriculum Guide For Grades 2-3   *Mufaro's Beautiful Daughters*

Tell pupils that first you will read the story together without stopping to take notes, and that you will then allow them to reread the story individually and take notes before discussing Manyara.

JUMP-IN READING

Use the oral reading method of jump-in reading to enhance pupil participation in the story. Start by reading part of the first page and pausing. Explain to pupils that when the reader pauses, another pupil should jump in and read some. When the second pupil pauses, another pupil should jump in and read, and so on. Monitor pupils so that they take turns and yield. Explain that a different person must read each time until everyone has read once.

Help pupils with vocabulary pronunciation and comprehension of unfamiliar words as needed.

After reading the story, review pupils' predictions and discuss how they match or do not match what the story was about.

Discuss the story and its meaning, ensuring that pupils understand difficult concepts.

Now, each of you will reread the story and make notes about Manyara. When everyone is finished, we will talk about Manyara, who she is, what she is like, and we will compare our notes.

Guide pupils in a discussion using their notes and the note-taking copy master at the end of this lesson.

As you reread the story, look and listen carefully for words, phrases, sentences that describe Manyara and tell you what she is really like, and what she believes is the true meaning of justice.

PART 3 BEYOND the Lesson

CROSS CURRICULAR LINKS

LANGUAGE ARTS

Have pupils write a poem about Manyara and her personal definition of justice. Pupils may wish to use the copy master at the end of this lesson called *I Know Manyara*.

GEOGRAPHY

Have pupils find Zimbabwe on the globe or map. In small groups, have them write a description of what they have learned about Zimbabwe from the globe or map, and what they learned of Zimbabwe from the story. Point out that the map shows them much that the story does not tell.

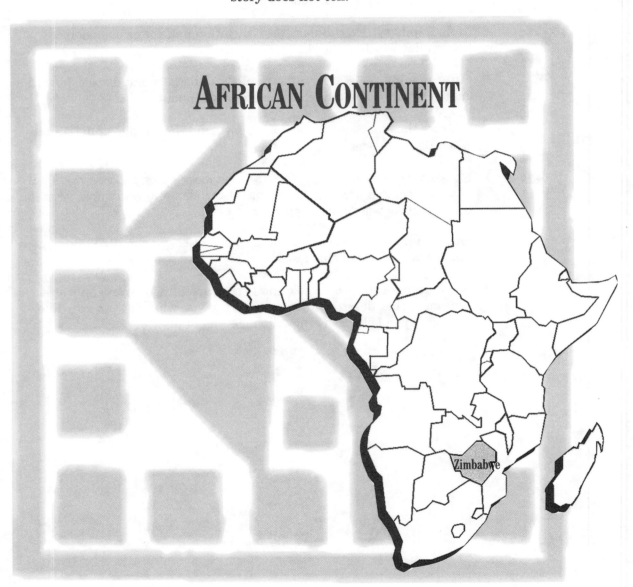

AFRICAN CONTINENT

Zimbabwe

Note-Taking on Story Characters

I Know Manyara

by _____

How Manyara Looks

1. _____

2. _____

3. _____

Important Things about What Manyara Hears and Says

1. _____

2. _____

3. _____

Important Things about What Manyara Feels

1. _____

2. _____

3. _____

Important Things about What Manyara Thinks

1. _____

2. _____

3. _____

What I Have Learned about Manyara

1. _____

2. _____

3. _____

4. _____

5. _____

POEM

I Know Manyara

by _____ Date_____

Manyara looks_____

_____

Manyara hears_____

_____

Manyara says_____

_____

Manyara thinks_____

Manyara feels_____

_____

Manyara is_____

_____

FANNIE LOU HAMER
AND THE FIGHT FOR THE VOTE
by Penny Colman

GOAL

Using the book *Fannie Lou Hamer and the Fight for The Vote*, **pupils will:**

develop **receptive language** in **Mainstream American English (MAE)** by:

- ▨ learning about the Civil Rights Era and Fannie Lou Hamer's contributions,
- ▨ using **jump-in reading techniques** to practice oral reading,
- ▨ communicating orally and in writing in **MAE**.

MATERIALS TO PREPARE

for each pupil in the group,

◉ a copy of the book *Fannie Lou Hamer and the Fight for the Vote*

to use with the group,

- ▨ at least one copy of the book *Fannie Lou Hamer and the Fight for the Vote*

Materials to Prepare for Cross Curricular Links

LANGUAGE ARTS	art paper, crayons and other art supplies
JOURNAL WRITING AND PERSONAL DICTIONARY	personal journals and personal dictionaries
MATHEMATICS	pupil access to data comparing the 1960s with today, e.g. African Americans in Congress or other public offices, graph paper, appropriater water-soluble markers
SOCIAL STUDIES	pupil library time for research, supplies for small group creative presentations
RESEARCH AND WRITING	pupil library time to locate additional books on Civil Rights figures, pupil journals, paper, pencil

PART 1 INTO the Lesson

INTRODUCTION

Discuss the concept of *struggle*.

How is struggle different from hard work?

Be sure that pupils understand the implications of the word struggle, i.e. hard work with an ongoing effort over a long time against opposition.

Have you ever had a struggle, really worked to learn or do something over a long time?

Encourage open discussion of pupils' struggles. Be sure not to violate the personal privacy of any pupil.

Did you know that during the 1950s, 1960s, and into the 1970s, a struggle for Civil Rights was fought by African Americans?

Discuss a *think, pair, share activity*: Ask children to think about a personal struggle combined with what happened to them and how they overcame it, then do a quick write about their personal struggle.

Discuss the Civil Rights Era. Ensure that pupils understand that laws in the U.S. combined with prejudice prevented African Americans from having full human rights. Discuss what civil rights are, i.e. the rights guaranteed to all Americans to be able to vote, get jobs, and live without being treated differently or with discrimination.

Discuss some of the rights people during the Civil Rights Era struggled for, i.e. Jim Crow Laws which blocked African Americans and other persons of color from voting, access to public facilities (buses, restaurants, swimming pools, clothing stores, etc.), little or no quality public education, etc.

Discuss how the gains of the struggle of the 1960s make the lives of African Americans today full.

PREREADING

Tell pupils that the story is about a real person named Fannie Lou Hamer. It is her true story during the Civil Rights struggle in the 1960s. Explain that Mrs. Fannie Lou Hamer was one of the mothers or beginning fighters of the movement.

Let's learn and sing Mrs. Hamer's favorite song *This Little Light of Mine, I'm Gonna Let It Shine.*

Teach pupils the song and let them enjoy singing.

Discuss the meaning of the song.
What does it mean to "let your light shine?"
What might Mrs. Hamer's "light" be?
What does letting your light shine have to do with the struggle for civil and human rights?

Show pupils the cover of the book and have them read the author's names.

JUMP-IN READING

Read the book using the jump-in reading method, in which you read the first page, then pause, and a different pupil jumps in to read some of the book, with another pupil jumping in when the reader pauses until all pupils have read.

Discuss the book, revisiting the concept of struggle and the Civil Rights struggle. Ask pupils to name other Civil Rights contributors. Encourage pupils to understand that everyday people made up the Civil Rights struggle and succeeded.

Have pupils identify **MAE** sentences and **AAL** sentences in the book. Ensure that pupils can restate AAL sentences as MAE and vice versa.

PART 3 BEYOND the Lesson

CROSS CURRICULAR LINKS

LANGUAGE ARTS

Have pupils create a class ABC book with a word and an illustration for each letter. Encourage pupils to use words that express the goals, ideals, and concepts of the Civil Rights Era. Encourage pupils to express their own collective values as a group, too.

JOURNAL WRITING AND PERSONAL DICTIONARY

Encourage pupils to write in their journals and to develop their own personal dictionaries of civil and human rights words.

MATHEMATICS

In small groups, have pupils research and prepare a chart comparing data from the sixties with today. Help pupils select appropriate topics, e.g. number of African American members of Congress, or serving as mayors or governors.

SOCIAL STUDIES

In small groups, have pupils research other people in the Civil Rights struggle. Have pupils prepare and present a poster or other creative presentation on the person. Encourage pupils to select a person about whom they know less, e.g. a local or state official.

RESEARCH

Encourage pupils to read other books on related subjects and report to the class or their group. You may wish to make this a small group project.

THE LION AND THE BULLS
by Aesop's Fables
Illustrated by Fritz Kredel

GOAL

Using the book *The Lion and the Bulls*, a fable by Aesop, pupils will:

demonstrate acquisition of **basic literacy skills** by:

- using pupils' personal multiple intelligence or learning modality strengths,
- developing writing skills by writing story endings,
- using contrastive analysis to compare **MAE** an **AAL**,
- using code-switching between **MAE** and **AAL**,
- encouraging a sense of unity by having pupils work in pairs or small groups,
- developing oral reading skills.

MATERIALS TO PREPARE

for each pupil in the group,

- copy of the **copy master** of African proverbs at the end of this lesson
- a copy of the Aesop fable *The Lion and the Bulls*

to use with the group,

- **class chart** or **chalkboard**
- if individual copies are not available, at least one classroom copy of *The Lion and the Bulls*

Materials to Prepare for Cross Curricular Links

LANGUAGE ARTS   paper and crayons for making group books

WRITING   copies of the copy master of African proverbs at the end of this lesson for each pupil and paper

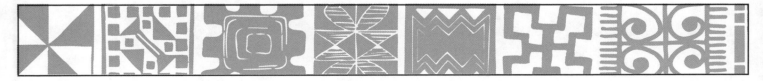

PART 1 INTO the Lesson

INTRODUCTION

Give each pupil a copy of the copy master at the end of this lesson. Explain to pupils that there are African proverbs on the sheet. Pair or group pupils and let each pair or group select one proverb.

Talk with your partner (group) about one proverb. Decide how you will explain your proverb's meaning to the class. Work with your partner (group) to prepare your explanation. It can be written, art, singing, dancing, oral— any kind of presentation that you choose.

Give pupils a designated amount of class time to prepare. Share each presentation with the class. As pupils begin working, be sure to encourage each pair (group) to utilize their strong learning modalities. You may wish to set up the pairs (groups) to have shared strengths in learning modalities, e.g. two artistic pupils collaborating.

When pupils give their presentations, encourage the class to conclude that there are many different types of learning strengths, and that all are valuable.

Next, discuss with pupils what a fable is. Explain who Aesop was. Explain that many fables came from Africa and that they usually are a story that teaches a lesson using animals as all or some of the characters.

JUMP-IN READING

Show pupils the covers and a few pages of the book. Encourage them to predict what the fable will be about. Write pupils' predictions on the class chart or chalkboard, and review them for accuracy and discussion after reading the story.

GUIDED READING

Have pupils help you read the story aloud. Remind pupils to take mental notes of story points they want to remember. Tell pupils to listen and think about the meaning of the fable, not just the characters and action. Encourage pupils who wish to to take written or pictorial notes during the story reading.

After reading the fable with the pupils, discuss it. Encourage both **MAE** and **AAL** in discussing the story. Model **MAE** for pupils. Discuss the moral of the fable.

Discuss how pupils' predictions matched or did not match what the fable was about.

PART 3 BEYOND the Lesson

CROSS CURRICULAR LINKS

LANGUAGE ARTS/DRAMA

In small groups, have pupils make up different endings for the fable. Pupils' endings may reflect the same moral or a different one. Have each group make a book of their fable ending, and provide time for each group to perform or present their version of the fable.

WRITING

Using code-switching, encourage individual pupils to rewrite a proverb from the copy master at the end of this lesson in **AAL**. Have pupils exchange their proverbs, and rewrite each proverb in **MAE**. Put both pupils names on the copy master.

The Lion and the Bulls

AFRICAN PROVERBS ON UNITY

African Proverbs on Unity listed below:

1. If you are in one boat you have to row together.

2. One finger can't wash your face.

3. We join together to make wise decisions, not foolish ones.

4. One person can't collect the crops.

5. One hand can't clap.

6. When you see a crow eating your neighbor's corn, drive it away or someday it will eat yours.

7. When the right hand washes the left hand and the left hand washes the right hand, BOTH hands are clean.

MISSISSIPPI CHALLENGE
by Mildred Pitts Walter

GOALS

Using the book *Mississippi Challenge*, pupils will:
acquire basic literacy skills by:

- reading and writing about the United States Constitution, and especially the 13th, 14th, and 15th Amendments.

MATERIALS TO PREPARE

for each pupil in the group,
- a copy of *Mississippi Challenge*
- a copy of *The Constitution Made Easier*, available from Peoples Publishing

to use with the group,
- a copy of the **U.S. Constitution** suitable for classroom display
- at least one classroom copy of *Mississippi Challenge*
- at least one classroom copy of *The Constitution Made Easier*, available from Peoples Publishing
- **class chart** or **chalkboard**

Materials to Prepare for Cross Curricular Links

LANGUAGE ARTS lined paper, art paper, crayons, and art supplies

MATHEMATICS time and resources to research data on people from the 1960s, graph paper, and water-soluble markers to create data graphs

SOCIAL STUDIES paper and art supplies to create a classroom timeline, paper and water-soluble markers for achievement charts comparing the 1960s with today

MUSIC CDs and tapes of Civil Rights struggle songs, tape recorder and, blank cassette for recording pupils struggle song

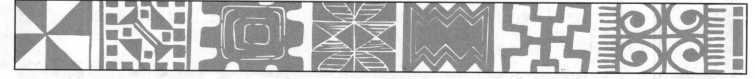

PART 1 INTO the Lesson

INTRODUCTION

Discuss the U.S. Constitution.

The Constitution is the most important document in our country because it tells all citizens what their rights are as Americans. The Constitution has been changed or *amended* over the years 27 times to take care of issues that were important and needed special attention, such as the right of everyone, including African Americans, to vote.

Show pupils a copy of the U.S. Constitution. Place it on the bulletin board or in another prominent classroom location. Then, tell pupils that they will make posters to explain three important parts of the Constitution.

Have pupils, working in small groups, make posters describing the 13th, 14th, and 15th Amendments. (Note: You may wish to have *The Constitution Made Easier* available to pupils. It is published by Peoples Publishing and is a brief, low reading level restatement of each bill and amendment. You may still have to help some pupils with vocabulary and concepts.)

PREREADING

Show pupils the book cover and interior. Have pupils predict what the book is about. Record pupil predictions and review them later for accuracy.

Be sure that pupils understand the book is about the struggle of African American people to obtain their civil rights. Pupils should be able to conclude that the book's setting is Mississippi. Help pupils understand that the book is about real historical events. Encourage sharing in group discussion of anything pupils already know about the Civil Rights Era.

PART 2 THROUGH the Lesson

SILENT AND GUIDED READING

Have pupils read one chapter of the book or a portion of a chapter silently or with partners, moving at their own pace. Encourage note-taking, in words or pictures, so that pupils can recall important events and people. You may wish to let pupils or pairs read different chapters and share with the group.

After pupils have read, discuss the book. Make a class list of the ways people worked to overcome injustice in Mississippi. Encourage pupils to share their chapters to enrich the understanding of the group.

Review important vocabulary to ensure that pupils understand the words.

Do you think that struggle made African Americans stronger? All Americans?

Discuss pupils' responses, encouraging critical thinking.

Have pupils read the entire book and write or give oral book reports.

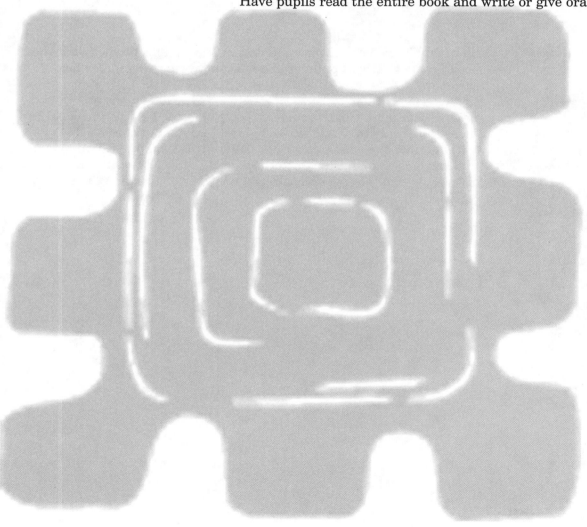

PART 3 BEYOND the Lesson

CROSS CURRICULAR LINKS

LANGUAGE ARTS

Have pupils write a summary of the achievements from the book, describing each and illustrating them. They may wish to make their own class achievement book.

Have pupils read the entire book and write or give oral book reports.

MATHEMATICS

Have pupils research and graph the numbers of people who contributed to the Civil Rights movement.

SOCIAL STUDIES

Have pupils make a classroom timeline of the events in the book.

Have pupils list the achievements of the 1960s from the book. Have them work in small groups to make a chart or display that compares and contrasts the gains of the 1960s with today. Encourage pupils to think critically about this comparison, looking for patterns, trends, and reversals.

MUSIC

Help pupils learn some of the struggle songs of this period by bringing in CDs and tapes. Pupils may want to write and perform their own struggle song. Tape record the class song for playback.

A GIFT OF HERITAGE:
HISTORIC BLACK WOMEN, VOLUME 1
by Empak Enterprises, Inc.
Illustrated by Steve Clay & S. Gaston Dobson

GOAL

Using the book *A Gift of Heritage: Historic Black Women, Volume 1*, pupils will:
develop an awareness and appreciation of language and cultural diversity by:
- identifying descriptive words in **MAE**,
- learning about notable African American women,
- expanding their personal thesauruses,
- creating a class time line,
- studying the biographical form as literature,
- writing biographies.

MATERIALS TO PREPARE

for each pupil in the group,
- copy of *A Gift of Heritage: Historic Black Women, Volume 1*, from Empak Publishing in Chicago, Ill.

to use with the group,

- *A Gift of Heritage: Historic Black Women, Volume 1*, by Empak Publishing
- chalkboard or class chart
- art paper for a class time line
- crayons and art supplies
- personal thesauruses

Materials to Prepare for Cross Curricular Links

LANGUAGE ARTS/WRITING	art supplies for illustrating their biographies, lined paper
PERSONAL THESAURUS	personal thesauruses, lined paper
MATHEMATICS	paper
SOCIAL STUDIES	time and resources to identify and learn about other African American women and their contributions
	art and other appropriate supplies for small group presentations of what pupils learned

INTRODUCTION

Discuss African American women whom pupils admire. These could be family relatives, friends, or famous personalities. Make a list on the class chart or chalkboard of descriptive words about them. Guide pupils to focus on important qualities, not "star" qualities.

PREREADING

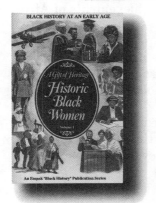

Have pupils look at the cover of the book. Help them identify the women. Encourage discussion about contributions women have made. Encourage pupils to use **MAE** in their discussions. If time is available, have pupils make a list of what they would like to learn about one of the women. Save the lists for use later.

PART 2 THROUGH the Lesson

GUIDED READING

Chose one or two of the biographies from *A Gift of Heritage: Historic Black Women, Volume 1,* and start reading aloud to pupils. Use the jump-in technique to have pupils help with the reading.

Discuss each story with pupils, ensuring that they understand the vocabulary and events. Discuss the issues confronting African American women. Discuss with pupils the achievements of African American women.

Encourage pupils to create a class time line placing women in chronological historical perspective. Encourage discussion of the people as pupils create the timeline, and model **MAE** for pupils.

Revisit pupils' lists of what they'd like to learn about the women. Provide library time to students, and class time to read aloud from the Empak book about the women in whom they are interested.

CROSS CURRICULAR LINKS

LANGUAGE ARTS/WRITING

Using their lists of traits of the women, have pupils write a brief biography of one woman. Have them support their thoughts by including both facts and opinions. Have pupils present their biographies to the class. Encourage use of **MAE**. You may wish to have pupils illustrate their biographies.

PERSONAL THESAURUS

Have pupils add their descriptive words about the women to their personal thesauruses.

MATHEMATICS

In small groups, have pupils use data, such as the years of events, to create word problems to solve. Pupils may focus on mathematical concepts such as the number of years that passed between two events, deciding how old a woman would be if she was a specific age on one specific date, and determining pupils' own ages depending on their year of birth (e.g. if they were born in the same year as one of the women or as one of the historical events). Have groups trade problems and solve each others' word problems.

SOCIAL STUDIES

Have pupils research other African American women and their contributions. You may wish to make this a small group activity and have presentations take any form pupils select.

TANYA'S REUNION
by Valerie Flournoy
Illustrated by Jerry Pinkney

GOAL
Using the book *Tanya's Reunion*, pupils will:
develop an awareness and appreciation of language and cultural diversity by:

- analyzing home language in the book,
- reading aloud,
- modeling Mainstream American English (MAE),
- engaging in written and oral expression of language,
- learning about the family histories of pupils in their class and the main character in the book,
- using contrastive analysis.

MATERIALS TO PREPARE
for each pupil in the group,

- a copy of the book *The Patchwork Quilt*
- a copy of the book *Tanya's Reunion*
- **paper**
- a copy of the **copy master** at the end of this lesson

to use with the group,

- book on tape version of the book
- tape recorder for playback
- chalkboard or class chart

Materials to Prepare for Cross Curricular Links

Language Arts	paper
Art	art supplies for making a mobile, such as clothing hangers and construction paper, nontoxic glue, safety scissors
Grandparent's Day	Prepare communication to grandparents or other older caregivers, family members and friends of pupils to share their family histories. Gather art supplies for a bulletin board sharing family histories.
Speaking	tape recorder for playback and recording, blank tape for recording

Tanya's Reunion

PART 1 INTO the Lesson

Note: *Tanya's Reunion* is a sequel by the same author to *The Patchwork Quilt*. It is suggested that pupils read *The Patchwork Quilt* for fun before doing this lesson on *Tanya's Reunion*. You may wish to give pupils time to read *The Patchwork Quilt* now and discuss the story and its characters.

INTRODUCTION

Who has attended a family reunion?
Tell us about a family reunion you have attended or heard about.

Give pupils time to share. Ensure that pupils understand the term family reunion.

QUICK WRITE

Have pupils Quick Write on the following topic, which you may wish to put on the chalkboard or class chart:

What are some of the feelings and fun you might expect to have at a family reunion?

Let pupils share their writing.

PREREADING

Conduct a picture walk through the book. Encourage discussion of the pictures, title, author, and illustrator. Encourage pupils to predict what will happen in the book and record their predictions for later evaluation after reading.

Tell pupils that Tanya has difficulty in adjusting to her new setting. Discuss feelings in new environments to which pupils can relate.

PART 2 THROUGH the Lesson

Tell pupils to listen as the book is read to distinguish between the family's home language and **MAE**. (Note: the nonmainstream speech patterns used in this story are not all reflective of **African American Language**)

GUIDED READING

If available, listen to the book on tape while pupils follow along. Stop the cassette at appropriate points in the story to explain difficult vocabulary and discuss the story. Then, conduct a Reader's Theater, with pupils reading parts of the book aloud.

Use the copy master at the end of this lesson to ensure that pupils understand the use of language in the book. Model **MAE** for pupils. Be sure that pupils interpret no negative feelings about the home language used by Tanya's family. Discuss appropriate uses of both home language and **MAE**.

CROSS CURRICULAR LINKS

LANGUAGE ARTS

Encourage pupils to write their own creative expressions to answer the questions Tanya asks her grandmother when she says, "This is your your history, isn't it, Grandma?"

Encourage pupils to write a story using both their home language and **MAE**. Encourage sharing.

ART

Have pupils make a mobile depicting Tanya's reunion.

GRANDPARENT'S DAY

Invite grandparents or other older caregivers, family members and friends to class to share their family histories. Afterward, have pupils make a bulletin board sharing their family histories.

SPEAKING

Tape record pupils speaking about their families. Then have cooperative learning groups or pupils working in pairs playback and analyze a speech, identifying **MAE** and non**MAE**. Ensure that negative judgments are not made.

TANYA'S REUNION

Write the Mainstream American English version of each phrase or sentence below.

1.   Got a card from Aunt Kay and Uncle John today.

_____

_____

2.   So I'm gonna go while I'm able.

_____

_____

3.   ....borned four of the first five Presidents of these United States.

_____

_____

4.   Until the bright, sunny sky grew cloudy and gray and the highway turned into never-ending dirt roads that seemed to disappear into the fields and trees, down into the the hollers, the valleys below.

_____

_____

5.   Can't you feel the place welcomin' ya?

_____

_____

6.   Watchin' you walk up that road, Rose Buchanan, ...

_____

_____

Name _____ Date _____

TANYA'S REUNION Cont'd...

7. Looks like it's comin' up a cloud,...

_____

_____

8. I think it's finally gonna rain!

_____

_____

9. I wanna go home, she murmured into her pillow.

_____

_____

10. Grandma, aren't we gonna bake today?

_____

_____

11. But here on the farm he's 'specially close,...

_____

_____

12. Race ya!

_____

_____

THE PATCHWORK QUILT
by Valerie Flournoy
Illustrated by Jerry Pinkey

GOAL
Using the book *The Patchwork Quilt*, pupils will:
recognize and label the **differences** between **African American Language (AAL)** and **Mainstream American English (MAE)** by:
- identifying and translating **AAL** and **MAE**,
- using contrastive analysis to identify and analyze **AAL** and **MAE**,
- practicing writing skills,
- using oral and silent reading techniques.

MATERIALS TO PREPARE
for each pupil in the group,
- a copy of *The Patchwork Quilt*
- **lined paper** for writing
- at least two different colors of **water-soluble markers**

to use with the group,
- at least one classroom copy of *The Patchwork Quilt*

MATERIALS to Prepare for Cross Curricular links
LANGUAGE ARTS	tape recorder and blank cassette
READING	the book *Tanya's Reunion*, also by Valerie Flournoy
DRAMA	lined paper
FAMILY INTERVIEW	lined paper

PART 1 INTO the Lesson

INTRODUCTION

Discuss keepsakes or special objects that have value to pupils. Allow pupils to share.

Now we will do a *quickwrite* activity. I will tell you something to write about, and will give you a short time, only five minutes, to write. At the end of the five minutes, we will share our writing.

The writing topic is: The Keepsake I Want to Pass On to My Grandchildren. Start writing now.

Time pupils for five minutes, then end the activity, allowing them to finish only the sentence they are writing when you call "**Time**."

Have pupils share their writing, encouraging respect and understanding of the special value of keepsakes in our lives.

Next, point out to pupils that sometimes **AAL** is used and sometimes **MAE** is used in their writing and speaking. Identify and have pupils reread or repeat **AAL** phrases/sentences and have the class translate them into **MAE**, and vice versa. Discuss appropriate use of home language and **MAE**. Encourage respect for both home languages and **MAE**.

PREREADING

Today we are going to read about a special family gift, a patchwork quilt.

Show pupils the book cover and have pupils read the names of the author, Valerie Flournoy, and illustrator, Jerry Pinkey.

As we read the story, notice the different types of language used to describe this special keepsake.

Show pupils the interior of the book and ask them to predict what will happen in the story. Write pupils' predictions on the board. Check their predictions after reading for accuracy.

PART 2 THROUGH the Lesson

GUIDED READING

Read the story aloud. You may wish to use a split group reading technique, with half the group reading every other page aloud. Encourage all pupils to read along.

Discuss the story to ensure that pupils understood vocabulary words and content. Encourage all pupils to enter the oral discussion and participate.

SILENT READING

Tell pupils that they may now reread the story silently. Tell them to notice different types of language, and to make notes of at least two different examples of **AAL**. When finished, use pupils' examples and have them translate into **MAE**. Have pupils use different color markers when writing in **AAL** and **MAE**. Work with pupils, giving positive feedback. You may wish to display pupils' work, or add it to pupil portfolios.

Continue the discussion, emphasizing that Tanya and her family had many special gifts, as all families do. Lead pupils to conclude that the objects are not as important as the values represented and passed on by and through them.

CROSS CURRICULAR LINKS

LANGUAGE ARTS

Have pupils role-play being a grandparent with their grandchild/children. Tape record them and play the recordings back to identify use of **AAL** and **MAE**. Give positive reinforcement for both.

READING

Encourage pupils to enjoy reading the sequel to *The Patchwork Quilt*, *Tanya's Reunion*.

DRAMA

Have pupils work in groups to write and act out a new ending or sequel to the story.

FAMILY INTERVIEW

Have pupils interview their parents, grandparents, or an older caregiver to learn about how they grew up, including their family and cultural customs and traditions. Encourage pupils to share these with the class in an oral presentation. To prepare, you may want pupils to write a set of questions that they will use.

WILLIE JEROME
by Alice Faye Duncan
Illustrated by Tyrone Geter

GOAL

Using the book *Willie Jerome*, pupils will:

recognize and label the **differences** between **African American Language** and **Mainstream American English** by:

- ▓ using contrastive analysis of **AAL** and **MAE**,
- ▓ using oral reading skills,
- ▓ using writing skills,
- ▓ reading literature reflecting pupils' home lives and personal and cultural interests as well as language.

MATERIALS TO PREPARE

for each pupil in the group,
▓ a copy of *Willie Jerome*

to use with the group,

- ▓ at least one copy of *Willie Jerome*
- ▓ **class chart** or **chalkboard**

Materials to Prepare for Cross Curricular Links

LANGUAGE ARTS — additional books with AAL sentences, pupil journals, and pupils' personal dictionaries

PERSONAL DICTIONARY — pupils' journals for developing personal dictionary

MUSIC — CDs or tapes of Winton Marsalis or another African American jazz musician, tape or CD player, art paper and supplies for pupils' creations

PART 1 INTO the Lesson

INTRODUCTION

Discuss with pupils the idea of passion (things we have great love for, things we spend a lot of time doing, things we deeply enjoy doing).

On the class chart or chalkboard, draw a semantic web for the word passion.
(Draw a circle in the center with the word passion written in it. Draw empty circles around the central circle. Connect the empty circles to each other and/or the central circle depending on their relationship to the additional concepts.)

Can you tell me some words that are related to passion? We will write your words in the empty circles.

Try to have at least one circle for each pupil response.

Discuss with pupils how their words connect and relate. Draw lines to connect the circles appropriately.

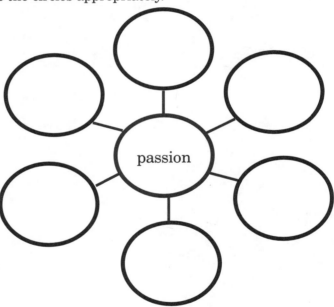

PREREADING

Show pupils the cover of the book. Have them predict what the story will be about.

Show pupils the interior of the book. Have them predict what they think Willie Jerome's passion is. Record predictions and check for accuracy after reading the book.

ECHO READING

Tell pupils you will read the book together by echo reading. Be sure that pupils understand the meaning of the word echo. Read each page and have pupils echo read it after you.

Discuss pupils' favorite parts of the book. Discuss what Willie Jerome's passion is.

Select several **AAL** sentences from the book and have pupils use contrastive analysis to restate them in **MAE**. You may wish to have pupils complete this activity in pairs.

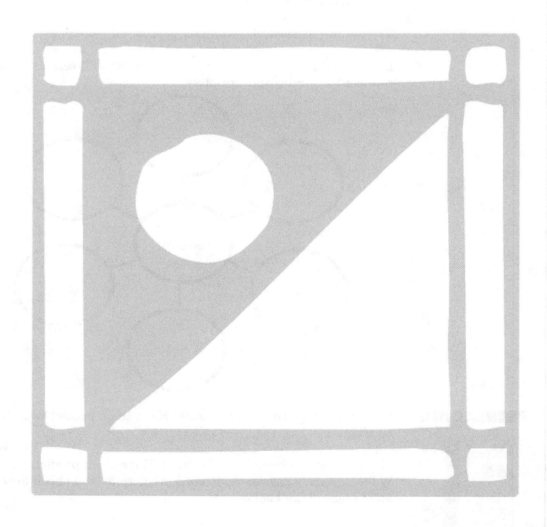

PART 3 BEYOND the Lesson

CROSS CURRICULAR LINKS

LANGUAGE ARTS
Have pupils read other books with **AAL** and perform contrastive analysis, translating **AAL** into **MAE**.

Encourage pupils to write in their journals and share their thoughts with partners. Journal writing may take any form, including poetry and fiction.

PERSONAL DICTIONARY
Encourage pupils to develop personal dictionaries of **AAL** words and terms with **MAE** translations.

MUSIC
Play some Winton Marsalis or other African American jazz music for pupils. Have them create a presentation (musical, art, poster, poem, etc.) expressing what they think the artist's passion is.

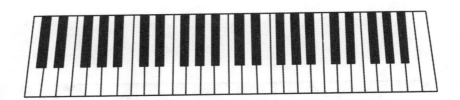

TAR BEACH
by Faith Ringgold

GOAL

Using the book *Tar Beach*, each pupil will:

expand a **personal thesaurus** of conceptually coded word concepts by:

- ▩ engaging in listening and speaking activities,
- ▩ reading and identifying words for inclusion in personal thesauruses,
- ▩ listening for new words to add to personal thesauruses.

MATERIALS TO PREPARE

for each pupil in the group,
- ◉ a copy of the book *Tar Beach*
- ◉ **butcher paper**
- ◉ art supplies for creating a quilt, such as **fabric**, **construction paper**, **colorful magazines**, and **wrapping paper**
- ◉ **nontoxic glue**
- ◉ **pupils' personal thesauruses**

to use with the group,
- ▩ **class chart** or **chalkboard**
- ▩ if possible, a **quilt**; if not, **colorful photographs of quilts**

Materials to Prepare for Cross Curricular Links

LANGUAGE ARTS   writing, paper, index cards cut in half to use as a deck of pupil-created cards, crayons or water-soluble markers to write on the cards, additional books on quilts for pupils to read such as *The Patchwork Quilt*, *Sweet Sara and the Freedom Quilt*, and *The Quilt Story*

MATHEMATICS   colorful art paper such as construction paper and magazines, safety scissors, non-toxic glue

INTRODUCTION

If possible, share a quilt with pupils, or bring in color photographs of quilts. Ask if pupils understand how quilts are made. Explain that quilts are pieced together from scraps of fabric, sometimes fabric that was left over from making clothing. Explain that quilts were created by women working together. Ask if pupils would like to make a classroom quilt or, if you prefer, pupils may create quilts in small groups. Examine the regularity of quilt design and the repetition of colorful patterns.

Have pupils discuss a quilt design and motif and draw their design so that it can be repeated regularly. You may want to encourage pupils to create stencils to use. Pupils will also need to measure the paper and their quilt squares to ensure that the pattern will fit correctly.

Using art supplies, large sheets of butcher paper, non-toxic glue, fabric and colorful paper, allow pupils to create a quilt.

PART 2 THROUGH the Lesson

PREREADING

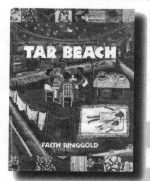

Conduct a picture walk through the book. Have pupils predict what the book will be about. Have pupils discuss similarities and differences between the book's cover and their classroom. Record pupils' predictions for review afterward.

Ask pupils if they have a favorite place at home, perhaps in their room or the kitchen. Talk about favorite places and the need for a personal place for reflection. Discuss why this is important. As pupils talk, write down key words on the chalkboard or class chart. Encourage pupils to include these words in their personal thesauruses with a definition and synonyms.

GUIDED READING

Have pupils read the book aloud, taking turns. After reading, review the book and discuss it to ensure that pupils understand the story.

Is the story like a quilt?

How did the author make her story a quilt?

Would you like to add words to your classroom quilt as the author did?

Give pupils time to add words to the quilt. Encourage discussion of which words to add and reflect on why they selected individual words and phrases.

Next, have pupils add the words to their personal thesauruses. Also, give pupils individual time to review the story and add other words to their personal thesauruses. Encourage pupils to share the words they added and discuss them.

Tar Beach

PART 3 BEYOND the Lesson

CROSS CURRICULAR LINKS   LANGUAGE ARTS

Writing
Have pupils write about their school or neighborhood using the image or metaphor of a quilt to describe it. Pupil writings may take the form of a poem or an essay. If pupils need help getting started, use the following starter sentence:

My school is like a quilt. It is _____.

Vocabulary
Have pairs of pupils create a synonym game as a deck of cards. Pupils start by making a list of some words from the story and then writing a synonym for each. Next, pupils can make a deck of synonym cards by writing each word on one card, its synonym on another card. Shuffle the cards and play a matching game similar to *"Go Fishing."* Allow pupils to make up the specific rules and enjoy their new game in pairs.

Literature
Have pupils find and read other books on quilts, creating a brief, written book report to give to the class. Suggestions: *The Patchwork Quilt, Sweet Sara and the Freedom Quilt,* and *The Quilt Story*. Have pupils add words from pupil reports to their personal thesauruses.

MATHEMATICS
Have pupils make a list of geometric shapes, discussing the differences among them. Then allow pupils to cut construction or other paper into the shapes and create a picture with them. Discuss how a collage is similar to and different from a quilt.

GRADES 2-3

MULTICULTURAL POETRY, ART, AND MUSIC

GOAL

Pupils will expand personal thesauruses **of conceptually coded words by:**

- experiencing and sharing poetry, art, and music from different cultures,
- writing about poetry, art, and music,
- exploring personal vocabularies,
- using oral and written language.

MATERIAL TO PREPARE

for each pupil in the group,
- **paper**
- **personal thesaurus** for each pupil

to use with the group,

- **chalkboard** or **class chart**
- as many examples of **culturally relevant art** as possible (use photographs where real examples are not available) in the following forms: painting, weaving, textiles, carving or folk art, sculpture, and drawing
- **African** and **African American music** and **equipment** for playing the music for pupils

Materials to Prepare for Cross Curricular Links

Language Arts Writing paper, and personal thesaurus for each pupil

Journal Writing pupil journals

Literature, Art, and Music books that include art and music as examples, such as:

Let's Make Music by Greenfield
Ty's One Man Band by Pitts
Willie Jerome by Duncan
Lift Every Voice and Sing illustrated by Gilcrest

Art art paper and supplies

Music You may wish to tape record pupil musical performances.

World Cultures Day preparations and refreshments to have visitors in for this special presentation day

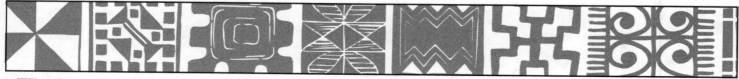

Multicultural Poetry, Art, and Music

PART 1 INTO the Lesson

INTRODUCTION

Today we will examine some of the contributions of African Americans and other people to poetry, music, and the visual arts. We will also search for new words to add to our personal thesauruses.

Remind pupils that a thesaurus is a collection of synonyms, and give examples from pupil thesauruses. Tell pupils that, as they write and take notes in this lesson, they should make note of words they want to add to their personal thesauruses.

Display as many examples of culturally relevant visual art including, but not limited to, painting, weaving, textiles, carving or folk art, sculpture, and drawing. Use photographs of the art to extend your classroom selection and display.

Encourage pupil discussion. Remind pupils of note-taking skills, have them create a chart with three headings: *Art, Poetry, and Music*. (You may wish to write these headings on the chalkboard or class chart.) Tell pupils to use their note-taking sheet to help them organize their thoughts. Then tell pupils to write down descriptive words under the appropriate heading as they continue this lesson. Give pupils time to view the visual art and record their notes. Give pupils time to share their notes in oral discussion.

Tell pupils they will now experience another art form—music. Tell pupils to close their eyes and listen as you play different types of African and African American music. Give pupils time to record descriptive words on their note-taking charts and time to share these. Discuss how the music and art make pupils feel, what touches them, and what they like best. Give pupils time to brainstorm words to describe the music and how they feel when listening to it.

Now, focus pupils on poetry. Allow time for pupils to use poetry books and anthologies and to go to the library to locate more poetry. Have each pupil identify one new poem, previously unknown to the pupil, to share with the class.

ORAL READING

Have each pupil read one short poem aloud. (If there is not enough time for this activity in the full class, divide pupils into small groups.) Discuss each poem briefly. Ensure that some poets read aloud in class are African American.

WRITING

Have pupils fill in their note-taking charts with descriptive words about poetry. Then, allow pupils to present their charts and discuss them. Have pupils fill in their personal thesauruses.

PART 3 BEYOND the Lesson

CROSS CURRICULAR LINKS   LANGUAGE ARTS

Writing

Have pupils work in small groups to write poems entitled *What Is Poetry?* using some of the words from their personal thesauruses. Have pupils highlight words they put into their personal thesauruses. Display the poems on the bulletin board.

Writing

Explain to pupils what a haiku is (a Japanese poetic form with a pattern of three lines in the following pattern: line 1-5 syllables, line 2-7 syllables, line 3-5 syllables). Have pupils write individual haikus and share with the class on an oral reading day. Use peer editing to help with pupil writing.

Journal Writing

Have pupils write in their journals about the art forms they have experienced in this lesson.

Literature, Art, and Music

Have pupils read books that include art and music as examples, such as

Let's Make Music by Greenfield
Ty's One Man Band by Pitts
Willie Jerome by Duncan
Lift Every Voice and Sing illustrated by Gilcrest

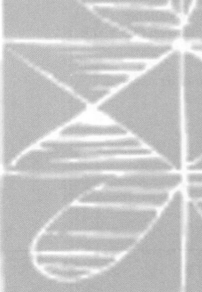

ART

Have pupils create their own interpretations of one art form in the lesson. Have pupils create works to express a new word or concept in the lesson.

MUSIC

Have pupils work in small groups to set their poems to music. Have the group select or write one poem, then work on singing the poem, set to music they create. Allow time for pupils to perform their works.

WORLD CULTURES DAY

Have a World Cultures Day on which pupils present art, literature, and music from around the world. Encourage pupil performances, choral readings, and sharing. Invite parents in to share the day.

FLOSSIE AND THE FOX
by Patricia C. McKissack
Illurstated by Rachel Isadora

GOAL

Using the book *Flossie and the Fox*, pupils will:

analyze linguistic differences between Mainstream American English (MAE) and African American Language (AAL) by:

- using contrastive analysis of **MAE** and **AAL**,
- comparing and contrasting language patterns of **MAE** and **AAL**,
- developing writing skills,
- developing personal vocabulary.

MATERIALS TO PREPARE

for each pupil in the group,
- a copy of the book ***Flossie and the Fox***
- **paper**

to use with the group,
- **chalkboard** or **class chart**
- at least one classroom **copy of the book** if individual pupil copies are not available

Materials to Prepare for Cross Curricular Links

LANGUAGE ARTS/WRITING	paper and pupil journals
MATHEMATICS	the alphabet chart created in the Vocabulary Development/Art activity, tape recorder, and blank cassette
LANGUAGE DEVELOPMENT/WRITING	tape recorder and blank cassette
VOCABULARY DEVELOPMENT/ART	crayons or other art materials and art paper

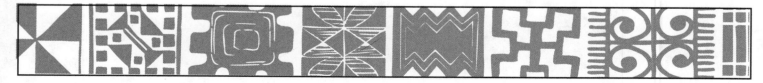

PART 1 INTO the Lesson

INTRODUCTION   Discuss language with pupils.

What is a language?
Is one language better than another?

Encourage pupils to understand that no language is better or worse than another.

How does a language help us?

Encourage pupils to understand that languages help us communicate. Encourage any other values and uses of language that pupils mention. Ensure that pupils realize that language can be written or spoken, and may even be nonverbal.

Write the following sentence on the chalkboard or class chart. Leave room to make a list of pupil responses under the blank line.

Chalkboard

Every language has _____.

Continue the discussion.

Are different languages spoken in our school?
Town?
What are some of the different languages used?

Encourage pupils to identify both **AAL** and **MAE** as languages. Discuss the differences in languages and their uses.

Encourage pupils to want to be multilingual. In small groups, have pupils create a list or presentation in any learning modality to explain why being multilingual is good.

PREREADING   Show pupils the cover of the book and encourage them to make predictions about the story. Write their predictions on the chalkboard or class chart and check the predictions after reading.

PART 2 THROUGH the Lesson

PREREADING

We will listen to a folktale that has different languages in it. Listen carefully for the languages of the folktale.

JUMP-IN READING

Read aloud the first page of *Flossie and the Fox*. Then have pupils read the rest of the story by using the jump-in reading technique.

Chalkboard

After reading, encourage pupils to share their analysis of the characters by writing one or two-word descriptors on the chart or chalkboard. Remind pupils to write the name of the character they are describing, or you may wish to allow pupils to draw the outline of the character and have the class identify who is being described.

Demonstrate contrastive analysis of **AAL** and **MAE** by selecting and reading aloud a sentence from the book in **AAL**. Have pupils recast the sentence in **MAE**. Discuss the differences in meaning and style.

Repeat this contrastive analysis activity going the other way, from **MAE** to **AAL**.

PART 3 BEYOND the Lesson

CROSS CURRICULAR LINKS

LANGUAGE ARTS/WRITING

Have pupils pretend they are Flossie and write about this time in their lives. Give pupils time for revising and editing their writing. Have pupils work in pairs to criticize each other's work verbally, then revise it to improve it.

Encourage pupils to write in their journals to express their reactions to the story.

MATHEMATICS

Use the alphabet activity below. Encourage pupils to devise songs or rhythmic oral presentations that teach addition, subtraction, or any other mathematical operation. For example, you might get pupils started with the following example of addition.

> J is letter 10.
>
> J is curvy, I like J.
>
> A is letter 1.
>
> A is straight, I like A.
>
> J and A are 10 and 1.
>
> Eleven, eleven, eleven.

LANGUAGE DEVELOPMENT/WRITING

Provide pupils with a tape recorder and blank tape, and let them record some phrases or sentences in both **MAE** and **AAL**. Play back each phrase or sentence. Stop and discuss whether it is **MAE** or **AAL**, and have pupils restate it in the other language. Continue until each pupil has recorded a phrase or sentence in **MAE**.

VOCABULARY DEVELOPMENT/ART

Have pupils make an illustrated alphabet, with a word they like for each letter. This may be an individual or group activity, depending on your wishes and time limitations. Tell pupils that they should use at least five words that were used in the story *Flossie and the Fox*. Extend the activity by encouraging pupils to write sentences and/or stories using as many of the alphabet words as possible. Encourage code-switching.

You may wish to record pupils' presentations for playback.

MIRANDY AND BROTHER WIND
by Patricia C. McKissack
illustrated by Jerry Pinkney

GOALS

Using the book *Mirandy and Brother Wind,* pupils will:

analyze linguistic differences between **Mainstream American English (MAE)** and **African American Language (AAL)** by:

developing pupils' appreciation of self and culture,

recognizing, comparing, and contrasting differences between **AAL** and **MAE**.

pupils will achieve these goals by:

- using literature that reflects the pupils' home life, personal interest, cultural background and/or language.
- using instructional conversations.

MATERIALS TO PREPARE

for each pupil in the group,

- a copy of the book ***Mirandy and Brother Wind*** (you may also want the accompanying audio cassette)

to use with the group

- if available, you may wish to locate a short **video** on a tornado or hurricane and show it to the group to start the discussion about wind. If so, you will need a **television** and **video player**
- **chalkboard** or **classroom chart**
- **tape player** and **audio tape** of music, preferably by African American artists
- **cards** with numbers, one per pupil (Do not repeat any number)
- **a cupcake** for each pupil (Be sure that you know any food allergies and have cupcakes or small cakes that all pupils can eat.)
- an **audio cassette recording** of the book ***Mirandy and Brother Wind***

Materials to Prepare for Cross Curricular Links

LANGUAGE ARTS copies of the book ***Mirandy and Brother Wind***, and, if you wish, the audio cassette version, paper, crayons, and writing journals

SCIENCE data on the wind speed during different seasons in your region. (This may be obtained by researching the issue at the library or contacting the National Weather Service or a local weather service.) graph paper and water-soluble markers for pupils to graph the data, a wind sock, and paper for recording wind sock results

MUSIC AND DANCE audio cassettes of music popular after the Civil War and during the turn of the century, costumes for pupils to dress up in like the clothing of the period of the book, i.e. post-Civil War to turn of the century

PART 1 INTO the Lesson

INTRODUCTION

If you wish, you may start the discussion by showing pupils a brief video about hurricanes or tornados.

How is a hurricane or tornado different from a windy day?

Help pupils distinguish between the wind of a hurricane, a tornado, a strong windy day, and a breeze.

How can you tell when there is wind?
What can you see that tells you whether there is wind or not?
How does the wind feel to you?
When it is a soft breeze?
When it is strong?
Has the wind ever felt so strong you had trouble walking?

Help pupils write a class "word wall" of words describing or telling about wind. You may use the chalkboard or a classroom chart.
Encourage pupils to generate descriptions of the wind in both **MAE** and **AAL**. Help them write both on the "word wall."

Who knows what a *cakewalk* is?
Have you ever heard any of your family or friends talk about a cakewalk?

If pupils are unfamiliar with the term, explain that it was a dance created by enslaved Africans. They danced, usually in couples, and the best dancers of the night won a cake. It was a way for enslaved people to express themselves in dance and celebration. Point out that the history of the cakewalk is African American.

Explain that another variation often played in the South in modern times, especially at local fairs, was to dance around in a circle on numbers on the floor. When the music stopped, the dancers stopped, and a number was called. If you were standing on the number called, you won a cake.

If you wish, you may let pupils participate in a cakewalk of their own. Give each pupil a card with a number, form a circle, and tell pupils to dance around in a circle while the music plays, stopping and holding their positions when the music stops. Then call out a number, and the pupil with the chosen number wins a cupcake. Be sure that all pupils receive cupcakes at the end of the activity.

PREREADING

Introduce the book to the pupils. Show pupils the cover.

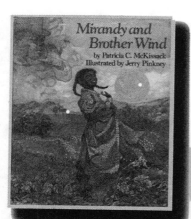

This book is called *Mirandy and Brother Wind*.

Can you read the author's name on the cover?
The illustrator?
What is an illustrator?

Help pupils read the author's and illustrator's names.

Show pupils some of the illustrations in the book. Ask pupils what period in history they think the book is about: today, ancient times, or a time closer to the time of slavery in the United States. Encourage pupils to notice the dress of the characters and the dance. Ask pupils if it could be a cakewalk. Encourage pupils to predict what the story will be about and when in time it might have occurred. You may wish to record pupils' predictions on the chalkboard or class chart for review after reading the story.

Mirandy and Brother Wind

PART 2 THROUGH the Lesson

GUIDED READING

Tell pupils that they will now read along with the story. Use the audio tape of the book if available, or read it to pupils yourself. In either case, stop the reading to discuss each page or section of the book. Tell pupils to notice when characters speak in **AAL** and when the author uses **MAE**.

Explain what a conjurer is if pupils do not know the word. Explain that it is a person who does magic. Ask pupils to look for what type of conjurer is in the story, and how the conjurer helps Mirandy.

As reading occurs, encourage pupils to read aloud with you or the tape. Stop after any page that some pupils do not seem to understand or with which they have difficulty. Read the entire story through once with pupils, ensuring that pupils understand the vocabulary and story line before asking pupils to read the story by themselves. Pupils may enjoy reading the story a second time. You may also want to keep classroom copies of the book and tape so that pupils may revisit it on their own.

Chalkboard

After reading the story through one time, discuss the language the characters use. Ask pupils if it is **AAL** or **MAE**. Have pupils look in their books and find examples of **AAL**. Write these on the chalkboard or class chart. Then, have pupils tell in **MAE** or their own words what the examples mean. Continue until each pupil has given and explained at least one example. Encourage pupils to use contrastive analysis (analyzing the differences and different uses of **AAL** and **MAE**) throughout the day by pointing out to you other examples of appropriate use of each.

Discuss the author's style.

Why did the author use **AAL** in this book?

Does the use of **AAL** make the characters seem real?

Encourage pupils to understand that the use of **AAL** makes the story more natural and realistic and the characters more alive. Encourage appreciation of the historical and cultural situations in the book, e.g. the cakewalk, the conjurer, and treating the wind as a person to make him seem real.

Ask pupils what they think about Mirandy's feelings towards Ezel. Ask pupils if she changed her mind by the end of the book. Ask pupils if they have ever changed their minds about someone. Discuss how important it is to be open-minded about other people. Discuss how we can learn things from other people. Pupils may wish to make a "word wall" of lessons they have learned from others.

PART 3 BEYOND the Lesson

CROSS CURRICULAR LINKS

LANGUAGE ARTS

Have pupils work in pairs or small groups and reread the book *Mirandy and Brother Wind*, stopping to make a list of some AAL expressions not already identified in the group activities. On a separate piece of paper, have pupils write five of the expressions, and for each write the MAE version. Also list missing or implied words from the AAL expression. Have each pair or group present their work to the class.

Writing Cinquain Poetry

Have pupils write a cinquain. Explain that cinque means five in French, and that a cinquain has five lines, as follows:

Line 1 — Subject, a noun
Line 2 — Two adjectives that describe the noun
Line 3 — Three verbs which tell what the noun does
Line 4 — Phrase which says something about the noun
Line 5 — Repeat of line 1 or a synonym

You may wish to write the above on the chalkboard for pupils to refer to. Encourage pupils to draw pictures on the page illustrating their cinquains, and display pupils' work.

SCIENCE

Help pupils research the wind during different seasons. From the library, bring in information from the National Weather Service or from a local weather service. Tell pupils data such as the highest wind during the past year in each season and the record highs. Help pupils plot these numbers on a graph.

Have pupils study wind direction by using a wind sock and recording their findings daily for a period of time, or for the entire year.

MUSIC AND DANCE

Obtain audio cassettes of music popular after the Civil War and during the turn of the century. Select some lively tunes and let pupils have their own historically accurate classroom cakewalk, with a "jury" of teachers or adults to decide on the best dancers. If you wish, allow pupils to dress up in costume.

OUR PEOPLE
by Angela Shelf Medearis
Illustrated by Michael Bryant

GOAL

Using the book, pupils will:

utilize Mainstream American English (MAE) structure functionally in oral and written form by:

- researching and writing about African American achievers,
- writing essays and in their journals,
- oral discussion of African American achievers.

MATERIALS TO PREPARE

for each pupil in the group,

- a copy of **Our People**
- **safety scissors**
- **art paper**
- **crayons** and **art supplies**, including people colors
- **personal journals**
- **writing paper**

to use with the group,

- a class copy of **Our People**
- **magazines** with African American achievers that pupils can cut up
- **sources of information** on African American achievers from which pupils can draw portraits and get information
- **authentic Kente cloth**
- **class chart** or **chalkboard**

MATERIALS to Prepare for Cross Curricular Links

LANGUAGE ARTS/WRITING	journals, paper, and personal dictionaries
SCIENCE, MATHEMATICS, AND TECHNOLOGY	time and resources to research and identify African American in these fields, art paper for creating posters, crayons, and art supplies
PERSONAL DICTIONARY	personal journals and personal dictionaries
WRITING	personal journals

PART 1 INTO the Lesson

INTRODUCTION

Introduce the concept of personal achievement. Discuss people that pupils think have achieved personal goals and have also contributed to our lives.

Encourage pupils to make a bulletin board of African American achievers whom they admire. Help with magazines that pupils can cut up and art supplies. Help pupils label the people they have selected and write a sentence to tell what each person has achieved.

PREREADING

Show pupils the Kente cloth. Explain that kente is woven by African men and boys in Ghana and other African countries. Explain that each Kente pattern has a different meaning. Discuss the artistic importance of patterns. Let pupils touch and examine the Kente. If possible, research the meaning of the Kente cloth that you have brought to use with the class and share its meaning with pupils. Then put the Kente aside.

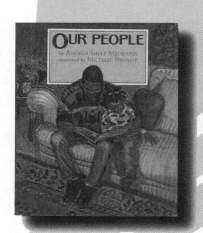

Today we will read a book about a special African American girl and her father. She learns from her father about the many contributions made by African Americans in our world today.

Show pupils the covers and interior of the book. Have pupils read the title and author's and illustrator's names to you. Have pupils predict what the story is about and what will happen. Write pupils' predictions on the class chart or chalkboard and review for accuracy after reading the book.

GUIDED READING

Have pupils help you read the story by jump-in reading or echo reading. Discuss the story as it unfolds, reinforcing positive shared traits of characters and pupils. Reinforce the story's emphasis on African American culture and self-esteem.

After reading, discuss and compare the African American achievers pupils put on their class bulletin board with those in the story. Guide pupils to continue learning more about African Americans.

Have pupils write group essays using one of the sentence starters below, which you may wish to put on the chalkboard.

African Americans have achieved much and continue to achieve.
Our most admired African American is _____ because . . .
The achievements of African Americans are especially impressive because . . .

Encourage pupils to understand that they, too, can achieve great personal goals.

PART 3 BEYOND the Lesson

CROSS CURRICULAR LINKS

LANGUAGE ARTS

Have pupils write about their own personal achievements in their journals. Have them write about both past and future achievements.

SCIENCE, MATHEMATICS, AND TECHNOLOGY

Have pupils research African American in these fields and create Achievement Posters with an image of the person/people and a written description in **MAE** describing their achievements. (Note: some appropriate materials for this activity are available from Peoples Publishing.) They are:

African Americans in Science, Mathematics, Medicine and Invention

by: The Rochester City School District

Ten Great African American Men of Science

With Hand-On Science Activities
by: Dr. Clifford Watson

African and African American Women of Science

Biographies and Hands-On Activities and Experiments
by: Leonard Bernstein,
Linda Zierdt-Warshaw,
and Alan Winkler

PERSONAL DICTIONARY

Have pupils add achievement words to their personal dictionaries and write **MAE** definitions.

WRITING

Have pupils practice code-switching by writing **AAL** sentences about achievement and translating them into **MAE**.

CARRY GO, BRING COME
by Vyanne Samuels
illustrated by Jennifer Northway

GOAL
Using the book *Carry Go, Bring Come*, pupils will:
demonstrate functional use of **Mainstream American English (MAE)** structure in oral and written forms by:

- ▓ engaging in verbal and written activities,
- ▓ reading aloud,
- ▓ using writing skills to write clear instructions in **MAE**,
- ▓ using oral skills by giving clear instructions in **MAE**.

MATERIALS TO PREPARE

for each pupil in the group,
- ✂ a copy of *Carry Go, Bring Come*
- ⊕ lined paper

to use with the group,
- ✂ if a copy is not available for each pupil, a class copy of *Carry Go, Bring Come*
- ▓ **task cards**, enough for each pair of pupils, each with a task written on it that pupil pairs must write instructions or directions for doing

Materials to Prepare for Cross Curricular Links

LANGUAGE ARTS	preparation for role playing using clear **MAE** directions
MATHEMATICS	lined paper
GEOGRAPHY	a globe or map of the world, task cards for pupils to write on, (one per group), and a compass rose drawn on the board

PART 1 INTO the Lesson

INTRODUCTION

Discuss how important it is to give clear instructions sometimes. Encourage pupils to talk about funny examples of times they misunderstood instructions.

Hand out the instruction task cards. A task is listed on each. Pupils are to work in pairs to write step-by-step directions for how to complete each task. Pupils are not to write the task on their direction/instruction sheet.

Have pupil pairs exchange their written directions. Have each pair read another pair's instructions aloud, and then deduce what the task is. Examine how the instructions could have been written to be more clear. Reinforce use of **MAE** in writing clear directions or instructions.

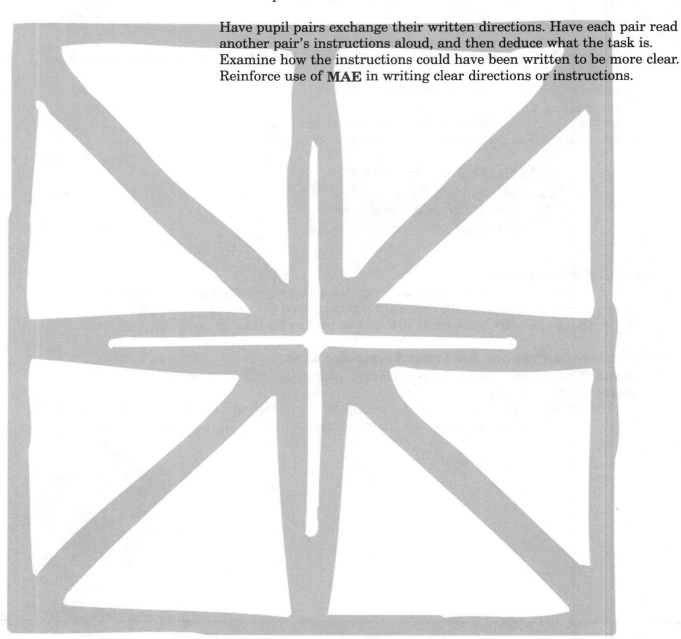

GUIDED READING

Carry Go Bring Come

Vyanne Samuels

Illustrated by Jennifer Northway

Have pupils read the story silently first.

Next, reread the story as a group, utilizing jump-in reading or echo reading.

Stop at each page and have pupils discuss what they would have done if they were Leon.

When finished with the book, have pupils make a class list of tips for writing good, clear **MAE** directions.

PART 3 BEYOND the Lesson

CROSS CURRICULAR LINKS

LANGUAGE ARTS

Have pupils role play giving clear **MAE** directions to another pupil. Some situations might be directions to the school office, directions on completing a common classroom activity, or directions on finding the lunchroom.

MATHEMATICS

Have pupils work in small groups to write a large number down, not sharing it with any other group. Next, have pupils write sequential directions for arriving at that number mathematically. Have groups exchange their word problems/directions and work them out, checking each others' math and accuracy in writing clear, sequential directions as a problem.

GEOGRAPHY

Have pupils find an African country in which they have an interest on a globe or map. In small groups, have them write directions for locating the country on a task card, being careful not to share the name of the country. Encourage pupils to use directions such as north, south, east and west. You may need to teach these concepts and draw a compass rose on the chalkboard. If pupils have difficulty, suggest that they can give directions from the U.S. or from other countries. Have groups exchange the cards and identify the correct countries from them.

LESSON ORGANIZER

To aid you in writing your own lessons,
we have provided this Lesson Organizer for you.
Please copy it and use it to organize your lessons
for your own classroom.

ENGLISH FOR YOUR SUCCESS *LESSON ORGANIZER*

LESSON TITLE _____

GRADE LEVEL _____

STRATEGIES AND APPROACHES

List the strategies and approaches by which the goal will be achieved.

STUDENT PRODUCT/CULMINATING TASK

What will students produce to demonstrate proficiency or achievement?

GOALS
(check one)

1. ☐ Acquire an awareness and appreciation of home language and culture

2. ☐ Develop receptive language in Mainstream American English

3. ☐ Acquire basic literacy skills

4. ☐ Develop an awareness and appreciation of language and cultural diversity

5. ☐ Be able to recognize and label the differences between African American Language and Mainstream American English

6. ☐ Expand a personal thesaurus of conceptually coded word concepts

7. ☐ Analyze linguistic differences between Mainstream American English and African American Language

8. ☐ Use Mainstream American English structure functionally in oral and written form

9. ☐ Recognize the language requirements of different situations

10. ☐ Demonstrate proficient use of Mainstream American English in written and oral form

11. ☐ Develop an expanded knowledge and appreciation of African American language and the languages and cultures of others

12. ☐ Communicate effectively in cross-cultural environments

Materials to Prepare

- **for each child in the group**

- **to use with the group or class**

Materials to Prepare for Cross Curricular Links

Curriculum Area	Materials

PART 1 *INTO* THE LESSON

TIME REQUIRED	INSTRUCTIONAL ACTIVITIES	STUDENT PRODUCTS/CULMINATING TASKS

Lesson Organizer

PART 2 *THROUGH* THE LESSON

TIME REQUIRED **DIRECTED(D) GUIDED(G) INDEPENDENT(I)** (LABEL EACH ACTIVITY)	INSTRUCTIONAL ACTIVITIES	STUDENT PRODUCTS/CULMINATING TASKS

PART 3 *BEYOND* THE LESSON

CURRICULUM OR ENRICHMENT AREA (LIST)	ACTIVITY

Lesson Organizer